Beep Beep THE ROAD RUNNER
A Very Scary Lesson

by Russell K. Schroeder

illustrated by
Phil DeLara and Bob Totten

GOLDEN PRESS • NEW YORK

Western Publishing Company, Inc., Racine, Wisconsin

NOPQRST

"Here, here! What's all this noise?" asked a startled voice from high atop a cactus. It was an elf owl, and he was annoyed at having been awakened so early in the day. Opening his sleepy eyes wide, he saw the Road Runner family below him, on their early-morning outing together.

A smile chased the cross look away. "Ah," he said, "a fine family you have there, Road Runner." Then he whispered, "I saw tracks last night. Be on the lookout for Wile E. Coyote!"

The Road Runners thanked him for the warning.

They knew all about Wile E. Coyote. That very morning, Papa Road Runner had lined up his children and told them how dangerous the coyote was. But then he had added:

"To stay safe inside,
Where the sun doesn't shine,
Makes a young bird pale and gray.
A Road Runner needs to beep and run—
So let's be on our way!"

And with a cheerful "Beep! Beep!" and a bob of their heads, they had set out on the day's adventure.

The yellow sun smiled down on them as they beeped good-bye to the friendly elf owl. If the owl's eyes hadn't closed in sleep that very minute, he might have noticed the shadow of a coyote following close behind the happy birds.

Soon the Road Runners reached some bubbling mud pits. A group of muddy tortoises lay there, basking in the sun and yawning contentedly.

"Want to join us in this lovely, squishy mud?" they asked.

"No, thank you," beeped the Road Runners, explaining:

"While some skim the clouds,
Some slide in the mud;
Each chooses the way he will play.
The Road Runner likes to beep and run,
So we'll be on our way!"

"Well, watch out for coyotes," yawned the turtles. They were too lazy to raise their heads, or they would have heard the stealthy padding of coyote feet close behind the Road Runner family.

Zipping along, with Papa proudly at the front, the children spied a creature they had never seen before. They dashed away from their father to meet this new creature on their own.

When Papa Road Runner glanced around and saw what had happened, he was startled. His children were fearlessly facing a mountain lion!

More quickly than it takes a frown to wrinkle your brow, he was at their side—and, just as quickly as a chuckle chases away a frown, he realized they had nothing to fear. This was a friendly mother mountain lion, and she was proudly showing off her two tiny yellow cubs.

"I'm surprised you let *your* children run around so freely," she said, giving one of her cubs a loving lick that sent him tumbling backward.

"If they didn't run, they wouldn't be Road Runners," Papa explained.

"You are right," Mother Mountain Lion replied. "And, of course, you've warned them about Wile E. Coyote. I'm sure I wouldn't want one of *my* precious babies wandering into his clutches."

For just a moment, the little Road Runners looked
nervously behind them, but the open desert beckoned
once more, and they ended their visit, saying:
    "Your friendship we value,
    And you have our promise
    We'll visit another day.
    But a Road Runner ought to beep and run,
    So we'll be on our way!"

If Mother Mountain Lion hadn't been busy separating her wrestling babies just then, perhaps she would have seen a coyote steadily trailing her new friends.

At the end of the trail, Papa Road Runner told the children they could explore on their own. He knew all Road Runners must learn to stand—and run—on their own two feet.

Peeking out from amid the rubble of a nearby junk pile, Wile E. Coyote's eyes lit up when he saw Papa Road Runner leave the three children.

He looked around the heaps of junk for something that would lure the unsuspecting little Road Runners to him.

"A bicycle horn! The very thing, if it beeps like a
Road Runner," he cried. But no. When he squeezed
the bulb, the sand-choked horn only wheezed.

He tried an auto horn. "A-*oo*-gah!" it blared. That would never do.

Then, inside a battered truck, he found a horn that sounded like a Road Runner. He crouched down in the seat and pressed the horn. "Beep! Beep!"

From far away, and then not so far away, he heard the answering beeps of the children.

Soon the little Road Runners were right beside
the truck. They were puzzled, for the beeping had
stopped.

At that moment, the truck door flew open, and out
jumped Wile E. Coyote! Here was the terrible fellow
the little Road Runners had been warned about! Their
legs whirled frantically, and the chase was on.

They raced over tires, leaped across a rusty bathtub, and scattered old magazines and newspapers. The coyote was right behind them. They climbed a mountain of furniture and bounced into a valley of bedsprings. Wile E. Coyote came closer every minute.

At last they dashed around the corner of the wrecked truck and leaped high, almost onto the back of Mother Mountain Lion, who was watching her cubs as they played.

Wile E. stopped in his tracks. This was a creature *he* feared. It took only one deep lion growl to send the sly coyote scurrying out of the junkyard and across the desert.

Papa Road Runner had been nearby, watching everything and ready to help if his children needed him. He knew they had learned a lesson about the tricks coyotes play.

"Thank you, Mother Mountain Lion," he said. Then he turned to his children. "We have one more place to go now." Smiling, he told them:

"When beeping and running
Have filled the whole day,
And stars twinkle overhead,
A Road Runner wishes, perhaps most of all,
To sleep in his own little bed."

And away the Road Runners ran, all in a line.